Special Thanks to Jodi, Shannon, Nick, and Sean

Willow Moon Publishing, 108 Saint Thomas Road, Lancaster, PA 17601,willow-moon-publishing.com

Cataloging Data
Nystrom, Hayley, The Fairies of Frost/ by Hayley Nystrom; illustrations by Alexandra Bulankina.
Summary: The Fairies of Frost introduces Lady Solstice and the magical fairies of winter..Hardcover
ISBN: 978-1-948256-23-0 Paperback ISBN: 978-1-948256-25-4 {1. Juvenile Fiction/Holidays and Celebrations. 2. Juvenile Fiction/Concepts and Seasons 3. Juvenile Fiction/Fairytales and Folklore 4. Stories in rhyme}

The Fairies of Frost

Written by
Hayley Nystrom

Illustrated by
Alexandra Bulankina

When the autumn air turns soggy,
And the sky is dark and gray

The Harvest Sprites grow groggy
They've finished with their play

Out comes Powder and her brother, Slush,
It's their turn to play again

Sledding down hills at a mad rush,
And building igloos, forts, and men

Twizzle, too, is out at last
Dancing across the ice
She zips and glides along real fast
Her leaps and twirls, so nice

By any glimmer, you'll find Shimmer
Seen twinkling near and far
He loves it so, the soft, warm glow
Of candle, light, and star

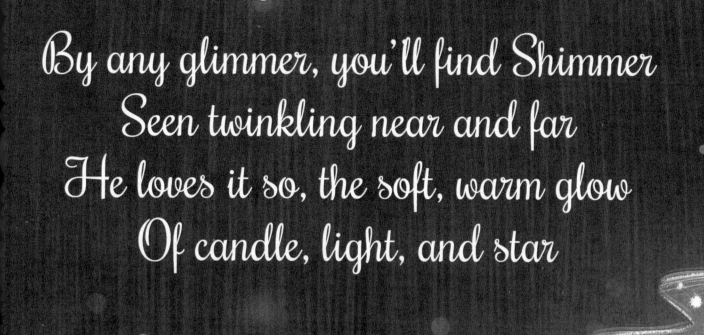

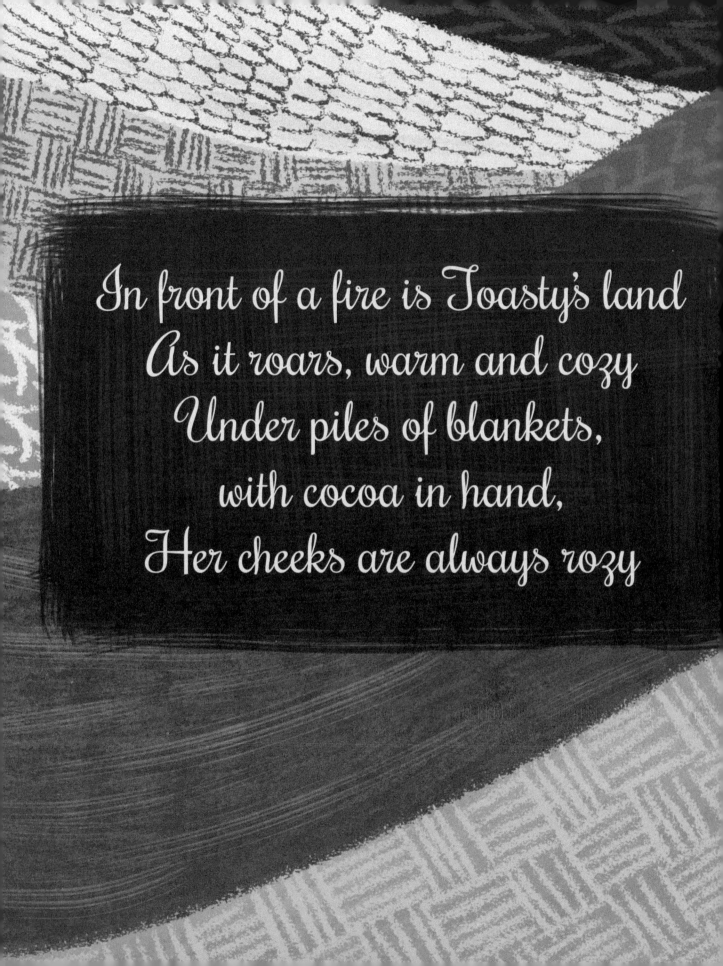

In front of a fire is Toasty's land
As it roars, warm and cozy
Under piles of blankets,
with cocoa in hand,
Her cheeks are always rozy

Never was a treat too sweet for Ginger to eat
Though she won't mind if you try
She'll take a bite of any delight
Be it cookie, cake, or pie

Banquet loves a hearty meal
With plates piled high as they're able
But knows the food only tastes ideal
With family and friends 'round the table

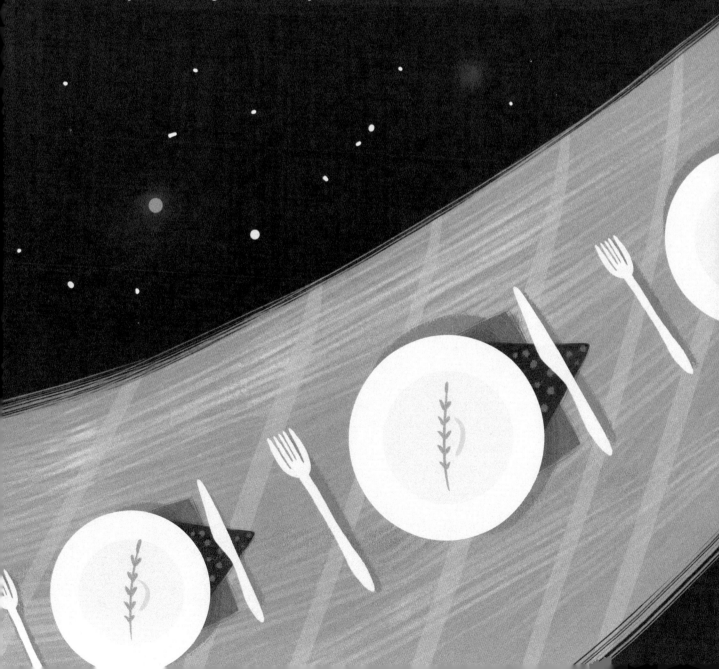

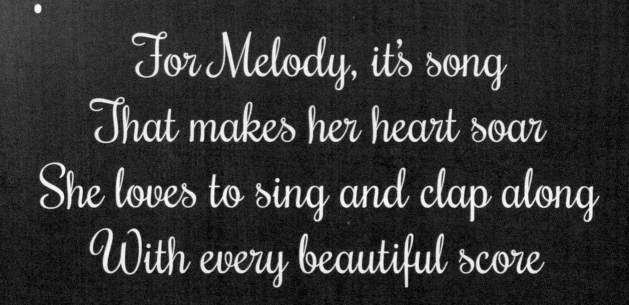

For Melody, it's song
That makes her heart soar
She loves to sing and clap along
With every beautiful score

Hush, on the other hand,
Likes when the songs cease
When stillness falls over the land
He is filled with calm and peace

Whether eating latkes or winning gelt,
Hallel stays for eight bright nights
The shimmering candles make hearts melt
During the Festival of Lights

Myrrh decks the halls with silver bells,
Trees, holly, and a manger
With goodwill on bless'd Noel,
No one is a stranger

For seven nights and seven days
Mazao has his fun
The drummers drum and candles blaze
So all may feel as one

You can count on Hourglass
To fill the world with cheer
They let the sweet stay and sour pass
At the stroke of new year

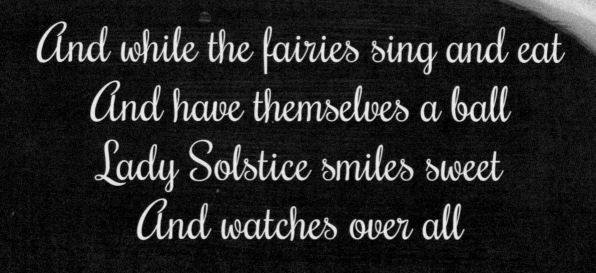

And while the fairies sing and eat
And have themselves a ball
Lady Solstice smiles sweet
And watches over all

So, down every road and river crossed
Through wood and desert, too
From Lady Solstice and the Fairies of Frost
A Happy Winter to you!

Meet the Author & Illustrator

Hayley is the author of The Fairies of Frost. She also works as an actress, singer and puppeteer. She's been performing since she was in her first dance recital at age 3, and holds a BA in Theatre. Hayley loves to utilize every medium she can to tell stories. She recently created the original shadow puppet piece, The Smith, The Hammer & The Doors of Notre Dame. When not writing or performing, Hayley likes to take French and swing dance classes with her husband, Sean. They live in New York City.

I'm an illustrator from Ukraine. I was fond of free-hand drawing from my childhood and during the period of higher education my hobby bit by bit was turning to my occupation. And, as a result, I became a digital illustrator. Therefore, now I'm able to share positive emotions and inspiration to lot of people through my illustrations, and it makes me really happy! You're welcome to my Instagram: https://www.instagram.com/sanches_art_

Made in the USA
Middletown, DE
26 October 2020